This project is sponsored by

Funded by Proposition 10

D0607190

Play with "o" and "g"

Library of Congress Cataloging-in-Publication Data
Moncure, Jane Belk.
Play with "o" and "g" / by Jane Belk Moncure ; illustrated by Colin King.
p. cm.
Summary: A brief tale showing how "o" and "g" can be
combined with other letters to form simple words.
ISBN 1-56766-936-0 (library bound)
[1. Alphabet.] I. King, Colin, ill. II. Title.
PZ7.M739 Pj 2001
[E]—dc21
00-010846

Play with "o" and "g"

Jane Belk Moncure

illustrated by Colin King

Starring the letters. . .

and

The publisher wishes to thank the letters "o" and "g."
Without them this book would not be possible.

This is little

This is little g.

and play.

What can we be?

This is little d.

May I play?

What can we three be?

Dog. Play dog.

Do what a dog can do.

We are little

and

May we play?

What can we four be?

Frog. Play frog.

Do what a frog can do.

What is that?

A frog on a dog.

What is that?

A dog on a frog!

This is little h.

May I play?

What can we three be?

Hog. Play hog.

What is that?

A frog on a hog.

This is little

May I play?

What can we three be?

Log. Play on a log.

A dog on a log.

Where is the frog?

A frog on a log!

Where is the dog?

What is that?

A hog on a log!

Good-bye, hog.

Good-bye, dog…and frog.

Good-bye, log.

Little  and also

play with and .

Can you?